In memory of Donald R. Smith, who loved to watch the waves
— L.C.

To Jim and Darlene Barrett
— J.L.

A mermaid!

THERE WAS AN OLD MERMAID WHO SWALLOWED A SHARK!

by Lucille Colandro

illustrated by Jared Lee

Scholastic Inc.

There was an old mermaid who
swallowed a shark.

I don't know why she swallowed the shark,
but it left no mark.

8

There was an old mermaid who
swallowed a squid.

That's what she did!
She swallowed a squid.

She swallowed the squid to float
with the shark.

I don't know why she swallowed the shark,
but it left no mark.

14

15

There was an old mermaid who swallowed a fish —
a tropical fish. That was her wish.

She swallowed the fish to dance with the squid.

She swallowed the squid to float with the shark.

I don't know why she swallowed the shark,

but it left no mark.

There was an old mermaid who swallowed an eel.

She let out a squeal
when she swallowed that eel.

She swallowed the eel to brighten the fish.
She swallowed the fish to dance with the squid.

She swallowed the squid to float with the shark.

I don't know why she swallowed the shark,

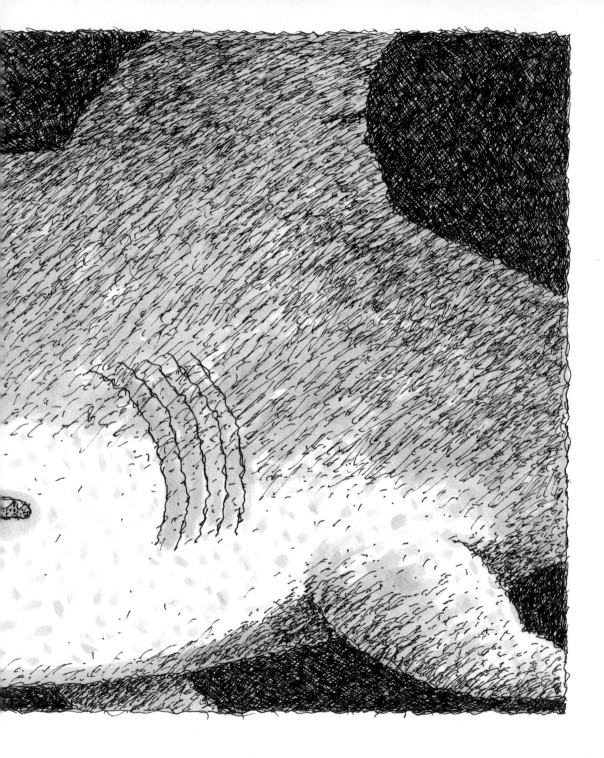

but it left no mark.

There was an old mermaid who swallowed a crab.
It was tough to grab, but she swallowed that crab.

She swallowed the crab to tickle the eel.
She swallowed the eel to brighten the fish.

She swallowed the fish to dance with the squid.

She swallowed the squid to float with the shark.

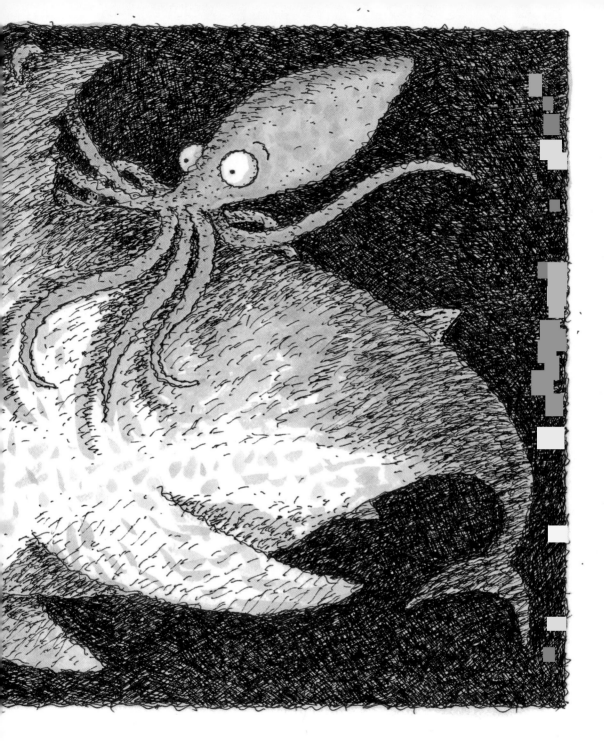

I don't know why she swallowed the shark,
but it left no mark.

There was an old mermaid who
swallowed a sea star.

She didn't swim far to swallow that star.

She swallowed the sea star to play with the crab.

She swallowed the crab to tickle the eel.
She swallowed the eel to brighten the fish.
She swallowed the fish to dance with the squid.

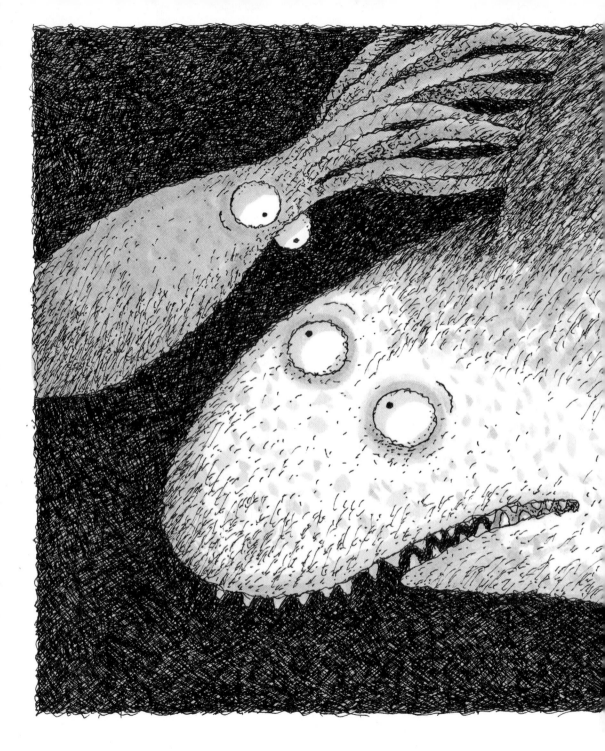

She swallowed the squid to float with the shark.

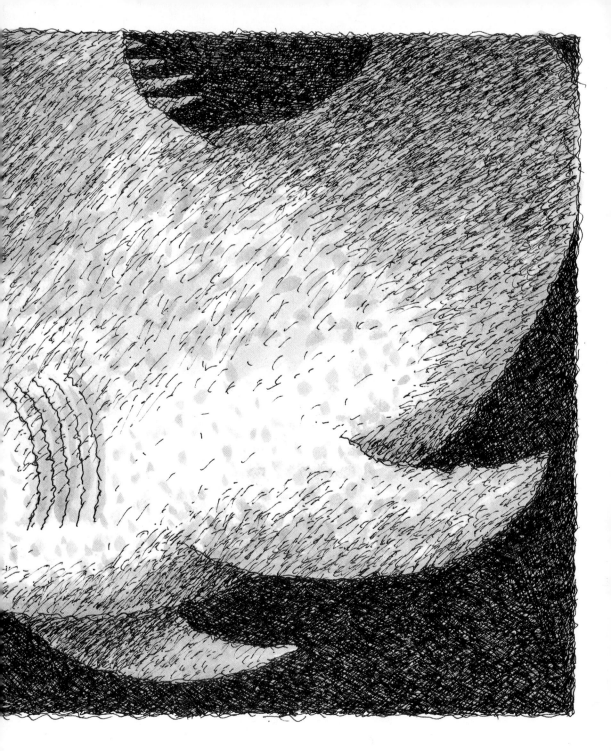

I don't know why she swallowed the shark,
but it left no mark.

There was an old mermaid who swallowed a clam.
It was fun to cram her mouth with a clam!

51

There was an old mermaid who loved to spend
her whole day playing pretend . . .

that everything under the water was her friend.

57

Sharks are born
with complete
sets of teeth and can
immediately get their own
food. Often when a shark
bites something, its teeth fall
out. But another tooth soon moves up
to take its place. Sharks can go through up to 50,000 teeth
in their lifetime!

Squid can swim as fast as twenty-five
miles per hour. They use jet propulsion.
Water squirts out of their bodies, creating a
force that helps them speed up. Many squid
live in the deepest parts of the ocean. The colossal
squid has giant eyes that light up so it can see the dark
ocean floor.

Tropical fish live in warm waters called the Tropics
around the world. Many tropical fish species are
brightly colored. That is why they are popular fish
to include in aquariums. About one
third of tropical fish species spend
some of their lives living in coral reefs.
These fish often help clean the reefs
by eating the plants growing on it.

Eels don't have scales. They are covered with a slimy substance that allows them to slither and slide. There are around 800 species of eels. Some species can live to be more than a hundred years old!

There are more than 10,000 species of **crabs**. A group of crabs is called a cast. Crabs have ten legs, but two of them are claws. They can use their claws to communicate with each other. Crabs often outgrow their hard shells. When that happens, a crab either molts and grows a new shell or it goes searching for a bigger shell to move into.

Sea stars do not have a brain or blood. These creatures can move quickly because of hundreds of tube feet on the underside of their arms. Sea stars usually have five arms that help them skim across tide pools. But some species can have up to forty arms! If one of a sea star's arms is injured, it grows a new one to take its place.

Clams have no eyes, ears, or noses, so they cannot see, hear, or smell. In order to protect themselves, they burrow deep in the sand in a group called a bed. There are more than 15,000 different species of clams. Some clams are small, but others can grow to more than 500 pounds! And some species can live up to forty years.

Search and Find!

The ocean is full of awesome creatures. Go back through the story and see if you can find the creatures listed below before the old mermaid swallows them, too! When you've found them all, check your answers with the answer key at the bottom.

Happy searching!

Barnacle

Lobster

Octopus

Shrimp

Conch

Whale

Dolphin

Sea lion

Clown fish

Sea horse

Angelfish

Sea turtle

Stingray

Sand dollar

Sea anemone

Oyster

Puffer fish/blowfish

Jellyfish

THERE WAS AN OLD MERMAID WHO SWALLOWED A SHARK!